This Book
Belongs To:

THE GINGERBREAD MAN
AND OTHER STORIES

from the
Best Loved Stories Collection

Copyright © 2004 by Dalmatian Press, LLC

All rights reserved
Printed in the U.S.A.

Cover Design by Bill Friedenreich

ISBN: 1-40370-747-2
13143-0604

04 05 06 07 08 LBM 10 9 8 7 6 5 4 3 2 1

Best Loved Stories Collection

THE
GINGERBREAD
MAN

AND OTHER STORIES

DALMATIAN PRESS

Table of Contents

The Gingerbread Man

Retold by Jackie Andrews

Illustrated by Terry Burton

Once upon a time, a little old man and a little old woman lived together in a little old house in the country.

Their children were all grown up and the little old man and the little old woman were lonely. So one day while she was baking, the old woman decided to make a little gingerbread man.

She rolled out the dough and cut it into the shape of a little gingerbread man. She gave him currants for eyes, raisins for buttons, and some red sugar for a mouth.

Then she put the pan into the oven to bake.
Later, when she thought it had baked long
enough, she opened the oven and took out the
little gingerbread man.

With a bump and a jump,
the gingerbread man leaped to
the floor. Out of the house he ran, calling back
over his shoulder, "Run, run, as fast as you can.
You can't catch me, I'm a gingerbread man."

The little old man and the little old woman ran out of the house and down the road after him, but they couldn't catch the gingerbread man. Soon he met a cat and the cat said, "Not so fast, little gingerbread man. I want to eat you."

The little gingerbread man ran on and, as he ran, he called back over his shoulder, "Run, run, as fast as you can. You can't catch me, I'm a gingerbread man." And the cat could not catch him!

So the little gingerbread man ran on until he met a dog, and the dog said, "Not so fast, little gingerbread man! I want to eat you!"

But the little gingerbread man only ran faster, and as he ran he called out, "I've run away from a little old woman and a little old man, a cat, and I can run away from you too, that I can!"

He skipped merrily along singing, "Run, run, as fast as you can. You can't catch me, I'm a gingerbread man!"

So he ran on and they all ran after him down the road, but they could not catch him.

By and by the gingerbread man met a cow in a field, and the cow said, "Not so fast, gingerbread man! I want to eat you."

But the little gingerbread man only ran faster, and as he ran he called out, "I've run away from a little old woman and a little old man, a cat, a dog, and I can run away from you too, that I can!"

And he skipped merrily down the road singing, "Run, run, as fast as you can. You can't catch me, I'm a gingerbread man!"

So he ran on and they all ran after him, but they could not catch him. By and by he met a pig and the pig said, "Stop, gingerbread man. I want to eat you!"

The gingerbread man ran on, and as he ran he called back over his shoulder, "I've run away from a little old woman and a little old man, a cat, a dog, a cow, and I can run away from you too, that I can!"

And he skipped merrily down the road singing, "Run, run as fast as you can. You can't catch me, I'm a gingerbread man!"

So he ran on and they all ran after him, but they could not catch him.

Soon the little old man and the little old woman had to stop, for they were completely out of breath and could not go a single step further.

Then the cat stopped, and the dog stopped, and the cow stopped, and they watched while the little gingerbread man and the pig ran on. But soon even the pig had to stop for a rest.

After a while the little gingerbread man passed
a fox sitting on a tree stump and he called out,
"Run, run, as fast as you can, you can't catch me,
I'm a gingerbread man."

The fox only laughed, so the little gingerbread
man sang out over his shoulder, "I've run away
from a little old woman and a little old man,
a cat, a dog, a cow, and a pig, and I can run away
from you too, that I can!"

The fox got up from the tree stump and he said, "But I don't want to catch you, so why do you run away from me?"

The little gingerbread man stopped running and the fox said, "Well, as long as we are going down the same road, don't you think we might as well walk along together?"

So they went on and on and after a while they came to the bank of a very wide stream.

The little gingerbread man looked this way and he looked that way, but there was no bridge across the stream.

"Just jump on my back," said the fox. "And I will help you across the stream."

So the little gingerbread man jumped on the fox's back and the fox started to swim across the water. After a while the stream got deeper, and the fox said, "Get up on my shoulders, little gingerbread man, or you will get all wet and melt away."

Once more the water got deeper and the fox said, "Now get up on my head, gingerbread man."

So the gingerbread man got up on the fox's head.

Snap! went the fox, and the gingerbread man was half gone. *Snap!* went the fox again, and the gingerbread man was all gone!

But that was all right—gingerbread men are made to be eaten, and the little old woman made another one the very next day!

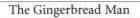

The End

The Chimp
and
the Fishermen

Retold by Val Biro

Illustrated by Val Biro

Once there was a
chimpanzee who lived
in the trees. Most
chimps do, because they like swinging from
branch to branch. This chimp had swung his
way through every tree in the jungle.

But he liked the palm trees best, because of
the coconuts. He would catch them as they fell,
then throw them up and catch them until they
fell on the ground and burst. That was the best
part because then he could drink the delicious
milk and eat the juicy white nut.

One day he looked into the river below the tree. He saw the fish swimming about and poking their noses into the air. He thought it would be nice to have some fish for supper.

"I wish I could catch some fish," he said, "but I don't know how. They don't fall off trees like coconuts do."

Just then two fishermen came along the riverbank. They were carrying a big net between them.

"Now, that is interesting. I wonder what they're going to do with a net?" thought the chimp.

"Perhaps it's for playing a game, like football or tennis." The chimp watched carefully to see what would happen next.

One of the men crossed the
river. Then the fishermen
stretched the net from one
side of the river to the other,
and let it drop into the water.

When the chimp saw this he realized it
wasn't a game after all. The net was for catching
the fish. What a good idea!

The fisherman who had crossed
the river came back to his friend.
"We should catch lots of fish," he said, and they
went off to wait in a shady spot round the bend
of the river.

At last the chimp knew about fishing.

"I shall try it for myself," he said, jumping down from the tree. "Why didn't I think of it before? All I need is a net, and then I shall have all the fish I want for my supper!"

And off he went to find a net.

He knew of an old hut nearby and ran to see what he could find there. Soon he found an old net and dragged it down to the river. It was very heavy but he didn't mind, as he was too excited about fishing and a fishy dinner.

When he got back to his tree, he tried to do the same as the fishermen had done. He tied one end of the net to a large branch, then jumped into the water with the net.

Poor chimpanzee! He couldn't swim. The net wrapped itself round his arms and legs and he struggled to get free, but he got so tangled up that he nearly drowned.

Just then the fishermen came back. "Look!"
said one of them. "There is a big furry fish
caught in the net! Did you ever see one like it?"
They laughed to see the silly chimp, but they
pulled him out of the river.

"Just remember," said one of them to the chimp, "there's more to catching fish than you think. You must learn about it first, before you try."

Then the fishermen walked off to see to their own net.

Realizing that what the fishermen said was true, the chimp ran back to his tree.

"I am not good at catching fish," he said. "But I am good at catching coconuts!"

And so that's what he did.

The End

The Lion
and
the Mouse

Retold by Val Biro

Illustrated by Val Biro

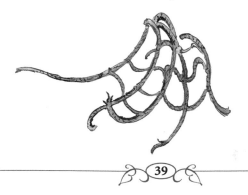

Once a lion caught a mouse. He wanted to eat it.

"This mouse is so small it's really not a very filling meal for me," said the lion, "but I might as well gobble it up anyway."

"Please let me go!" cried the mouse. "Be kind to me and one day I will help you."

That was a funny thing to say because how could a tiny mouse ever help a big strong lion? It sounded ridiculous!

The lion laughed. "How could a little mouse ever help me?" But he let the mouse go because the mouse was brave enough to speak to him. Besides, the lion wasn't very hungry anyway. The mouse squeaked his thanks and scampered away.

Later, when the lion grew hungry, he went hunting in the forest. He did not know that some hunters had set a trap for him. He fell right in! The lion roared with anger. All the animals in the forest ran away from the terrible noise—except one.

The mouse heard the lion's roar and ran to help. He knew that the lion was in trouble, and he remembered the promise he had made when the lion had let him go.

The mouse saw that the lion was caught in a net made of strong ropes. With his sharp little teeth the mouse bit through the net. It was hard work and took a long time, but the mouse went on nibbling until at last he made a big hole in the net.

The lion was free! He climbed out of the trap and smiled his thanks at the mouse. The mouse sat down and smiled back at the lion. You see, a mouse can help a lion!

And from that day on the mouse and the lion were the best of friends.

The End

The Little Red Hen and the Wheat

Retold by Jackie Andrews

Illustrated by Lesley Smith

Once there was a little red hen who lived in a big farmyard with her three fluffy yellow chicks. A dog, a cat, and a pig lived in the farmyard, too.

One fine morning, as she was busily scratching about the yard looking for something to eat, the little red hen found some grains of wheat.

"Look! Look!" she cried in great excitement. "See what I have found! Who will help me plant these grains of wheat?"

"Not I," said the dog. "I have some very important bones to look after."

"Not I," said the cat, "for I have visitors coming in a few minutes."

"Not I," said the pig. "I don't know how to do things like that."

"I'll do it then," said the little red hen.

She scratched and scratched until she made some holes in the ground and she put in the grains of wheat. The chicks covered them lightly with earth. After a few days, some little green shoots appeared.

The wheat grew and grew.

"Now, who will water the wheat?" asked the little red hen one day.

"Not I," said the dog. "I have some other things to do today."

"Not I," said the cat. "I have to take a little nap in the sun."

"Not I," said the pig. "I must go and cool off in the shade."

"I'll do it then," said the little red hen, and she did.

The little chicks helped her carry water, and the wheat grew and grew.

One day the little red hen asked, "Now, who is going to weed this wheat?"

"Not I," said the dog. "That kind of work doesn't agree with me."

"Not I," said the cat. "I would not be able to tell the weeds from the wheat."

"Not I," said the pig. "I have so many other things to do."

"I'll do it then," said the little red hen, and she did.

After some time the wheat turned yellow and began to ripen.

The dog and the cat and the pig came to admire it.

"What fine wheat we have," they said.

"Yes, indeed, it is time to reap the wheat," said the little red hen. "Who would like to reap it for us?"

"Not I," said the dog.

"Not I," said the cat.

"Not I," said the pig.

"I'll do it then," said the little red hen, and she did.

She carefully took off each precious head of wheat and put it in a bag held open by the three chicks.

"There," she said at last, and she called again to the dog, and the cat, and the pig.

"Who will take this wheat to the mill to be ground into flour?" she asked.

"Not I," said the dog. "The dust would get into my nose and make me sneeze."

"Not I," said the cat. "You know I cannot carry such a heavy load."

"Not I," said the pig. "Why, I do not even know where the mill is."

"Well, I'll do it then," said the little red hen, and she did.

The little chicks helped her and she carried the wheat off to the mill. The miller took the wheat and ground it into fine flour, and the little red hen carried it back to the farmyard.

The dog and the cat and the pig came to see the fine flour.

"Now, who is going to make this flour into bread?" asked the little red hen.

"Not I," said the dog. "I don't know how to make bread."

"Not I," said the cat, "I can't make bread either."

"Not I," said the pig. "I've never made a loaf of bread in my life."

The little red hen looked at them.

"I'll do it then," said the little red hen, and she did.

She measured, she mixed, she stirred and she kneaded, and soon the loaf was ready for the oven.

But first she had to have some wood to make a good hot fire. She called the cat and the dog and the pig once more.

"Who will help me to gather wood to build a fire?" she asked them.

"Not I," said the dog.
"Not I," said the cat.
"Not I," said the pig.
"I'll do it then," said the little red hen.

She carried wood, and she made a fire, and when everything was ready she asked, "Now, who is going to bake this bread?"

"Not I," said the dog.

"Not I," said the cat.

"Not I," said the pig.

"I'll do it then," said the little red hen, and she put the loaf of bread in the oven to bake.

When the loaf was baked, it was beautiful, golden brown, and crusty—and it smelled ever so good. The little red hen put it on the kitchen table, and the dog and the cat and the pig came and looked at it hungrily.

"Well, now, who is going to eat this bread?" asked the little red hen.

"I will," said the dog quickly.

"I will," said the cat, coming closer.

"I will," said the pig, pushing right up to the table.

"Oh, no, you won't," said the little red hen. "You didn't help me with any of the work. So my little chicks and I are going to eat it."

She called her chicks together, and they ate it all—every bit!

The End

The Farmer and His Sons

Retold by Val Biro

Illustrated by Val Biro

An old farmer worked hard all his life. He grew big, juicy grapes in his vineyard. They were big and juicy because the old man worked so hard, digging and forking and hoeing carefully around every vine.

When the grapes were ripe, he sold them at the market. People paid a lot of money for such wonderful grapes. But the old farmer was not happy. He was a very worried man.

The old farmer had three sons. They were all very lazy. They never did any work, not a scrap. They had no idea how important it is to work hard.

The three sons just lay in the shade all day, leaving all the work to their father.

The old farmer wanted his sons to do well. He wanted to teach them how to be good farmers.

So one day the farmer said, "There is a great treasure baried in my vineyard. You must remember this when I die."

The sons' eyes lit up! The old man saw how interested his sons were in finding the treasure.

When the old farmer died, his sons
remembered what he had said. Of course
they remembered! There was hidden treasure
in the vineyard. They were very excited. They
thought about bags of gold, sacks of coins, and
chests bulging with silver and pearls.

All they had to do was dig for it.
"Let us find the treasure," they cried, and
ran out into the vineyard. They set to work
immediately with spade, hoe and fork.

They dug hard and looked all over the vineyard for the treasure. They hoed out the weeds in case the pearls were hidden under them. They turned over the hard soil with their forks

looking for gold and coins.

They dug deep with their spades in the hope of finding a bulging treasure chest. And they carried on digging, week after week.

They worked very hard for a long time, but not a penny could they find. Not a single pearl or a nugget of gold. Absolutely nothing! And they had worked over every bit of the vineyard.

"Father must have been playing a trick on us," they said. "There is certainly no treasure in this vineyard."

So they gave up work and just lay in the shade. They were very disappointed.

But by now the vineyard was so well dug that the grapes soon grew big and juicy. It was a dry, bad season for other farmers, but not for the three sons. Their grapes were better than any that had ever been grown before.

When the grapes were ripe, the sons took them to the town to sell in the market.

Everybody crowded round to see such marvelous grapes. In a short while, the sons sold all the grapes and their pockets were full of money.

The sons were amazed. "The grapes are the treasure from the vineyard," they said. "Hard work will bring us treasure."

Their father was right after all. He had taught them how to be good farmers, and they worked hard in the vineyard from then on.

The End

Old
MacDonald
Had a Farm

Retold by Jackie Andrews

Illustrated by John Bennett

Old MacDonald had a farm, E-I-E-I-O!

And on that farm he had some cows, E-I-E-I-O!
With a moo-moo here, a moo-moo there,
Here a moo, there a moo, everywhere a moo-moo.
Old MacDonald had a farm, E-I-E-I-O!

Old MacDonald had a farm, E-I-E-I-O!
And on that farm he had some sheep, E-I-E-I-O!

With a baa-baa here, a baa-baa there,
Here a baa, there a baa, everywhere a baa-baa.

A moo-moo here, a moo-moo there,
Here a moo, there a moo, everywhere a moo-moo.

Old MacDonald had a farm, E-I-E-I-O!

Old MacDonald had a farm, E-I-E-I-O!
And on that farm he had some pigs, E-I-E-I-O!
With an oink-oink here, an oink-oink there,
Here an oink, there an oink,
    everywhere an oink-oink.

A baa-baa here, a baa-baa there,
Here a baa, there a baa, everywhere a baa-baa.
A moo-moo here, a moo-moo there,
Here a moo, there a moo, everywhere a moo-moo.
Old MacDonald had a farm, E-I-E-I-O!

Old MacDonald had a farm, E-I-E-I-O!
And on that farm he had some ducks, E-I-E-I-O!

With a quack-quack here, a quack-quack there,
Here a quack, there a quack,
       everywhere a quack-quack.

An oink-oink here, an oink-oink there,
Here an oink, there an oink,
    everywhere an oink-oink.
A baa-baa here, a baa-baa there,
Here a baa, there a baa, everywhere a baa-baa.

A moo-moo here, a moo-moo there,
Here a moo, there a moo, everywhere a moo-moo.
Old MacDonald had a farm, E-I-E-I-O!

Old MacDonald had a farm, E-I-E-I-O!
And on that farm he had some hens, E-I-E-I-O!
With a cluck-cluck here, a cluck-cluck there,
Here a cluck, there a cluck,
      everywhere a cluck-cluck.

A quack-quack here, a quack-quack there,
Here a quack, there a quack,
       everywhere a quack-quack.
An oink-oink here, an oink-oink there,
Here an oink, there an oink,
       everywhere an oink-oink.

A baa-baa here, a baa-baa there,
Here a baa, there a baa, everywhere a baa-baa.
A moo-moo here, a moo-moo there,
Here a moo, there a moo, everywhere a moo-moo.
Old MacDonald had a farm, E-I-E-I-O!

Old MacDonald had a farm, E-I-E-I-O!
And on that farm he had some dogs, E-I-E-I-O!
With a woof-woof here, a woof-woof there,
Here a woof, there a woof,
    everywhere a woof-woof.

A cluck-cluck here, a cluck-cluck there,
Here a cluck, there a cluck,
  everywhere a cluck-cluck.
A quack-quack here, a quack-quack there,
Here a quack, there a quack,
  everywhere a quack-quack.
An oink-oink here, an oink-oink there,
Here an oink, there an oink,
  everywhere an oink-oink.
A baa-baa here, a baa-baa there,
Here a baa, there a baa, everywhere a baa-baa.
And a moo-moo here, a moo-moo there,
Here a moo, there a moo, everywhere a moo-moo.
  Old MacDonald had a farm, E-I-E-I-O!

The End

The Ducks
and
the Tortoise

Retold by Val Biro

Illustrated by Val Biro

A tortoise was tired of crawling. Walking made him very tired and running was quite impossible. The house on his back was big and heavy and his four stumpy legs were short and weak—so he crawled everywhere very slowly.

He could swim, but being underwater became boring after a while. What he really wanted was to see the great big world from above.

"I wish I could fly like the ducks!" he said.

When the ducks landed nearby, he crawled over to them. "Will you teach me to fly?" he asked.

"You can't fly without wings," said the ducks. "Anyway, you are quite the wrong shape with that big round house on your back and those short stubby legs. You would look ridiculous."

But the tortoise begged and pleaded with the ducks.

After a while the ducks got tired of this silly, pestering tortoise and decided to teach him a lesson.

"You can't fly up into the sky just like that," said one of them. "But we can take you up on this stick. Hold it in your mouth."

The ducks took hold of the stick at each end and the tortoise grabbed it in the middle. Then the ducks spread their wings and up they all flew.

They flew over a village. The people were amazed to see a tortoise in the air. Who had ever seen such a thing?

It was such a strange sight that they stared and waved their arms. The tortoise saw the people waving and it made him very proud.

"They must think that I am a very clever tortoise," he thought. Yes, he was the only tortoise in the world who could fly, and he had to tell them.

"Look, I can fly!" the tortoise shouted, opening his mouth, which was not a very clever thing to do!

When the tortoise opened his mouth, he let go of the stick and down he fell. ***Thump!***

That's the end of the story, except that the tortoise decided that flying wasn't such a good thing after all, at least not for tortoises!

The End